ABRA**X**US TASKER COLLEGE
SENIOR YEAR

Extra
CREDIT

ABRAXUS TASKER COLLEGE
SENIOR YEAR

Extra
CREDIT

Ali Whippe

4 Horsemen
Publications, Inc.

4 Horsemen Publications, Inc.
1497 Main St. Suite 169
Dunedin, FL 34698
4horsemenpublications.com
info@4horsemenpublications.com

Cover & Typesetting by Battle Goddess Productions

Ebook ISBN: 978-1-64450-121-4

Paperback ISBN: 978-1-64450-122-1

DEDICATION

For every "Hot For Teacher" Fantasy

ustin Cooper looks from his phone to his gym teacher and back again.

"Midterm grades are posted online," Coach Smith says, "and I'll be in my office if anyone has any questions. Otherwise, you're done for the day! Go home." She pauses, then adds, "Don't forget to support the Stallions at the game Friday night." Most of the class stands immediately, grabbing bags and checking phones as they wander out of the room.

Justin stares at the grade on his phone, face heating as he takes in what it says. *C,* he thinks frantically. *I cannot have a C. My GPA cannot take a C, especially for something as stupid as gym. I shouldn't even have to take gym in college anyway—dodgeball is for high school.*

Not that they actually played dodgeball in gym class. Well, maybe they did—he hasn't been to class often enough to notice what they do when they aren't in the actual classroom with desks. He thinks they go outside and run around the track sometimes. He always sneaks away at that point. He thought his vanishing act had gone unnoticed, but the C tells him otherwise.

Justin smirks, gearing up to face the Coach. He is charming. He knows how to do this. A few words, a few smiles, and that C will be an A in no time.

Coach Smith may run the athletics department at Abraxus Tasker College, and she may be in charge of the best football team the school has had in years, but she's still just a tiny red-headed woman. Justin is sure he can charm her.

He stands up after everyone else has left the room, debating which way to go to her office. He can cut through the locker room, which will probably be empty this time of morning since the teams don't usually practice until the afternoon, or he can go around through the hallway and come from the other side of the building. Justin decides that he doesn't want to walk around, just in case any other students are waiting in the hall to speak to the coach. From the locker room, he can see if anyone is there and wait out of sight until they leave. He doesn't want her to expect him, to prepare herself to see him. He knows he is sexy, knows that his female teachers are susceptible to flattery, and he's not above using the advantage of his good looks to get his way.

His twin sister Jamie can be the righteous one, insisting on earning her grades. Justin knows that given grades are far sweeter than earned grades, and he checks himself in the locker room mirror once more.

His face is handsome, strong cheekbones and black hair, dark eyes and sexy lips, and his body is just muscled enough to impress without being overbearing. He is young and strong and often sexy. This should be easy.

He knocks on the door to the coach's office, waiting for her low voice to tell him to enter before opening the door. Tightening his muscles to present a strong core, he steps into the room confidently, shutting the door behind him so no one else can hear their conversation. The closed blinds over the window rattle as the door closes, the sound loud as he turns around.

Coach Smith sits behind a metal desk covered in binders and papers, a computer monitor nearly buried in the chaos. Two chairs sit in front of her desk, and she gestures for him to sit in one of them. He obeys, looking behind her at the shelves of trophies, most of them decades old. The chair is comfortable as he sinks into it, and he resists the urge to sag. *It's gym class,* he reminds himself. *I need to show her I'm already in shape.*

"So Mr. Cooper," Coach Smith says, "what brings you to my office?"

"I wanted to talk about my grade," he begins, leaning forward with a charming smile.

"Of course you do," she sighs, grabbing a pile of papers and shuffling through it. She finds the page she is looking for and scans it with a delicate finger. "Ah yes, that's why."

"Why what?" he prompts.

"You have a 71%," she says. "That's a C." After a pause, she adds, "You realize that C is a gift, right? You're barely out of D range." She looks up. "You do know that class runs until 10:45?"

Justin nods. "Yeah."

"I wasn't sure," she comments, "since you tend to disappear around 10." She frowns at him. "I don't think I've ever seen you on the track, Mr. Cooper."

"I don't think I need to be on the track to stay in shape, Coach Smith," he replies, leaning forward to stretch out a toned forearm and rest it on the edge of her desk.

"The point of this class isn't about keeping your shape," she says, arching an eyebrow.

"Then what is the point of gym class in college?" he asks. He realizes it's the wrong thing to say immediately, watching as her eyes narrow at him.

"You might know that if you'd ever actually looked at the syllabus," she says tartly, glancing over his shoulder at the clock above the door.

Justin knows he has to do something quickly before he loses control of the conversation completely.

"I know that the syllabus covers the grade breakdown," he says quickly, "but it doesn't mention your extra credit policy."

Coach Smith looks at him again. "You angling for extra credit, Mr. Cooper?" she asks. "How original."

"So you've done it before," he presses.

"You mean let students do something completely extra that I then have to grade instead of just doing whatever the class assignments were?" she asks sweetly, her annoyance bleeding through the words.

"I can do anything," he offers, smiling just enough to suggest how far he is willing to go. "Anything you need."

She glances around the room. "I'm afraid I don't find myself needing anything at the moment," she says finally. She cocks her head. "I did need you to stay in class the whole time," she comments. She squints at him, face suddenly speculative. "Are you always a quick deserter or do you ever go the distance?"

Justin stares at her, mouth falling open. *Did she just...?*

Coach Smith chuckles, "That's what I thought." She looks him up and down, those bright eyes lingering on the lines of his shoulders and chest. "No doubt you always finish in a hurry," she tells him.

"I've never had any complaints," he defends himself, his bruised ego rallying. "I go the exact distance I need to go."

She scoffs. "Hardly." She pins him with a glare normally reserved for lazy athletes. "I bet you can't even manage to get me anywhere without losing it first." She sighs wistfully, looking over him at the clock again. "I really feel for some of these college girls," she admits, "stuck with such eager selfish boys."

"I can go the distance," Justin says, leaning forward now, face determined. "I can get you there and back again easily. No problem."

Coach Smith smiles at him, leaning back in her chair and spreading her legs suggestively. The short skirt she wears rides up to reveal delightfully creamy thighs, her skin smooth and taut. She puts one foot up on the edge of the desk, her sneaker pressed against the metal, and the skirt slides up even more, just enough to reveal her bare pussy to his suddenly lustful gaze.

"No problem?" she echoes, running a finger down her body to skim across her exposed skin. "You think you can get me off twice before you lose it?"

Justin bites his lip, nodding eagerly. He's always wanted to fuck Coach Smith. The tiny redhead has featured in more than one of his highlight reels. He glances over his shoulder at the closed door behind him, then over at the blinds pulled down over the glass window into the hallway. They are alone.

He scoots forward off the chair onto his knees, crawling behind the desk to kneel in front of her chair, aware of how she watches his body move across the floor, cool eyes assessing his muscles. He looks down at her bare pussy, the skin smooth and waxed. He's wondered if she is a true redhead since the first time he saw her months ago. Now he will never know.

"So what do I get if I succeed?" he asks, reaching out a hand to stroke her left leg, fingers sliding from the top of her socks, over her muscled calf, behind her knee, and lingering against her inner thigh.

Coach Smith smirks at him. "Tell you what," she says. "Get me off twice before you come, and I will just give you that A."

Justin lets his fingers slide up to graze the top of her clit, eyes focused on her expression. He nods, "Done."

"But if you don't," she adds, eyes pinning his, "you have to be my mascot for the rest of the season."

Justin's fingers falter, a frown crossing his handsome face. "What?"

"You heard me," Coach Smith says, grabbing his hand and pressing it against her clit, positioning his finger right where she wants it. "I need someone to be the mascot at the games," she tells him. "That's you."

Justin smirks, "But only if I come before you do." He leans forward, his free hand moving up her other leg, confident fingers finding her opening and sliding across her sensitive skin.

Coach Smith nods, "That's right." She lets go of his hand, reaching out to lift up his shirt instead, fingers opening the button of his jeans and pulling the zipper down.

"But—" Justin sputters, but then she is tugging his semi-hard cock from his boxers, small fingers wrapping around him in a way that makes him close his eyes and moan. He catches himself, then opens his eyes and bites his lip. "That's not fair," he accuses.

Coach Smith strokes his cock again, one hand focusing on the head and the other slipping down to cup his balls. "Who said this would be fair?" she breathes, a challenge in her eyes. "You need to earn at least twenty percent more for your grade here. That shouldn't be easy."

Justin rallies, and it is clear he knows his business, at least in theory, because he immediately goes to work with both hands, his thumb slowly stroking her clit in round lazy circles and his other fingers slide back and forth against her opening. "You are so wet," he moans, the thought making his cock get even harder in her grip. He wants to bury himself in that pussy, to pound her until the coach screams his name. But this is a challenge, and he means to succeed. Trying to focus around her hands on his cock, he watches her face for clues, reading the way her mouth opens in a low moan of pleasure as he continues to rub her clit, the red flush working its way up her chest as he slides one finger inside her.

"You make me wet," she tells him encouragingly. "But can you make me come?"

"Oh yeah, baby," he promises, shifting so that he has two fingers inside of her and rubs her clit with his thumb, his other hands pushing her shirt up, the purple and silver Stallions tank top revealing small but perky breasts with hard nipples. He leans forward to suck a nipple into his mouth, letting his other hand continue up to her neck and then her jaw, sliding a finger into her mouth. She sucks the finger, eagerly tasting herself on his skin, and presses against him, clearly wanting more. The rhythm on his cock falters, and he focuses, adding a third finger and increasing the speed of his thumb, keeping the pressure the same. He moves to the other nipple, sucking hard, and then moves up to trace the edge of her jaw.

She rocks against his hand, biting her lip, one hand abandoning his balls and sliding up to grab his neck, the other continuing that same sultry rhythm at the head of his cock. He needs to distract her from that, or he's going to lose this bet before he even begins.

"You like that?" he asks, kissing along her jaw, moving his hand faster. She scoots forward, body moving against him now.

"That's nice," she admits, opening her eyes to look at him, "Very nice." She moans, but the sound isn't right. She's enjoying herself, no doubt, but there's no more build up. Justin knows he will have to try a new angle.

"But you need more," he tells her, his mouth finding hers and sucking her lower lip into his. His tongue brushes against hers, skilled and eager. "I have more for you, baby."

"You better," she tells him, "or you're my mascot." She pauses. "Maybe you'll fuck better in the costume."

"I don't need a costume for this." He grins, kissing down her chin and neck, taking a moment to suck each nipple on his way down, then he leans forward to bury his face between her thighs. She loses her grip on his cock, finally breaking the rhythm that was going to break him, as he slides down onto the floor. He keeps his fingers moving inside her, gently sliding back and forth, and he sucks her clit, first hard then gently, the alternating rhythm eliciting gasps of pleasure from the coach.

"Oh fuck!" she says. "You do know how to lick pussy!"

He grins against her skin, unable to stop himself, feeling a little bit of pre-cum dribble out of the end of his cock at her words. He does have some skills, he thinks, tongue working in that same rhythm, loving how her little body is tight with eagerness. He feels the orgasm build, her pussy tightening around his fingers, body shuddering against him. He continues sucking on her clit for another moment while she moans, "Oh yes, Mr. Cooper!"

One down, he thinks. *One to go*. His cock is dripping. He pauses for a short moment breathing against her skin, then licks her again, knowing she will be sensitive. He leans forward to suck on her clit again, but she scoots forward, pushing off the chair and standing, her pussy pink and swollen but above him now. She crooks her finger, gesturing for him to stand up. He obeys, his pants pooling around his ankles, cock hard at attention. He wants to reach for her, knowing he could lift her easily, bring her down on his cock and fuck his way to glory.

But I need that A. Not yet, he tells himself. *One more*.

"Nicely done," she says, "but can you do it under duress?"

He raises an eyebrow, a hand absently pumping his cock as he stands in front of her. "What do you have in mind?"

She looks him over with a critical eye. "You say you don't need gym class," she says, "because you're already fit?"

Justin shrugs, knowing his body is nice to look at, but he is also strong and in shape. He could run on the track, but he just doesn't want to, preferring to run on the treadmill in the air conditioning at the gym with his music in his ears, not sweating under the sun with his classmates. "I am," he says. "What do you have in mind?" He imagines her climbing him like a tree, impaling that sweet pussy on his aching cock, breasts bouncing as she rides him like a wild woman, red hair a messy curtain around her flushed face.

"A challenge," she says, sliding her skirt and shirt off quickly. Justin takes off his shirt, dropping it onto her abandoned chair as she reaches for him. For a second, he thinks she is going to do exactly what he has been hoping, but instead of settling her legs around his hips, she turns him around so she stands next to his right side. She pats his shoulder to make sure he is steady on his feet, then reaches out to place both of her hands on top of his right shoulder. Like a cheerleader starting the bottom of a tower formation, she launches herself up with a bounce and lands on his shoulder in a surprising display of agility and strength, one leg against his chest and the other touching his back.

For a moment, she hovers there, her wet pussy pressed against his skin, and then she slowly slides around to his front, one thigh on either side of his face, her legs tucked over his shoulders and her pussy right in front of his mouth. She looks down at him, grinning, a hand on the back of his head. "You good so far?"

"Oh yeah," he says, tongue reaching out to lick her clit right in front of him, hands gripping that fantastic ass. He is strong enough to hold her like this for a while.

"Good," she says, "now hold on to me." His hands grip her ass and then slide to her waist and hips as she slowly leans back and down, body facing away from him to give him a great view of her breasts as she dangles from his shoulders like a cheerleader about to flip. But instead of lifting her legs from his shoulders and bouncing away from him, she lets herself straighten out upside down, making sure he has a good hold on her hips, her back pressed against his chest and stomach.

Justin moves her forward a little bit, angling her body so his tongue can reach all of the best parts of her. He is just settling into this new position, when the coach shifts, twisting her upper body around so that one hand grips his right thigh and her other hand cups his balls while warmth enfolds his cock. He freezes, hips jerking forward involuntarily as she sucks him deep into her warm mouth, his tongue slipping back into his mouth as he moans. She pulls him close again, this time squeezing his balls in a steady rhythm to match her mouth, and Justin knows he isn't going to make it.

He leans forward, diving into her pussy with his tongue, but she keeps sucking his cock in that perfect rhythm, hands pressing his balls in the same motion. He pulls her hips forward again, burying his tongue in her, and while he knows that she is close to coming again, there is no way he is going to outlast that mouth on his cock.

His mind races through possible ways to stop himself from coming, all of the things that could stop the wave of pleasure, but her mouth is moving in a way that makes him see stars, and he steps awkwardly back, leaning his butt against her desk. A binder crashes to the floor but he ignores it, licking her pussy with everything in him.

The wave builds even higher, and he knows he won't be able to hold it.

How bad could the mascot really be? Justin decides he can suffer through a few games in a silly suit if only he can come in that magic mouth right now.

He lets go with a moan, sucking her clit in a last desperate effort, and then he collapses onto the desk behind him, careful not to bend his body too much and hurt the coach as she sucks the orgasm out of him. She uses a hand on the desk to prop herself up, then easily sits up in front of his face. She looks down at him, a hand in his hair as she swallows, licking a finger suggestively.

"Oh no," she croons, shaking her head. "Like I thought, too soon across the finish line."

"That was a dirty trick," he says against her pussy, tongue snaking out to lick her again.

"That was just a blowjob," she tells him.

"I've had blowjobs," Justin says. "That was...athletics."

Coach Smith snorts, lifting a leg off his shoulder and climbing off of him. "I am the Director of Athletics," she reminds him. "You should expect that kind of thing." She steps back into her skirt, then slides her tank top over her head, shaking her hair out over the neck. Justin leans down to pull up his pants, grabs his shirt from where he abandoned it on the chair, and stands there, still catching his breath.

"So," Coach Smith says dismissively, leaning down to pick up the binder from the floor and adding it to the top of a haphazard pile near the edge. "Game is Friday at 7. I expect you in the locker room at 6."

2

*J*ustin Cooper stares at the mascot costume laid out on the bench, debating how to begin. He glances hopefully at the few guys in the locker room with him. They've probably seen people put this on before. Maybe they can help.

He picks up the bottom, studying the structure of the costume. He's wearing gym shorts and a tank top, so it should be easy enough to slide the pants over his legs. Stepping into one leg, he wobbles a little, arm reaching out to catch his balance on the bench, but a strong arm grabs his shoulder and holds him steady.

Justin looks over his shoulder to see Aaron, the quarterback for the XTC Stallions grinning at him. "You got roped into the mascot, huh?" he asks, nodding sympathetically. "What did you do to piss someone off?"

"It's extra credit," Justin tells him. "For gym."

Aaron nods slowly, a flash of understanding passing between them. "Coach can be a real hardass sometimes," he says. "Very demanding woman." He bites his lip, shaking his head as his eyes go distant, lost in memory. Seeming to return to the moment, he gestures with his chin. "I'll hold you up. Once you get the other leg on and get the shoulders the right length, you should be fine." He holds Justin's shoulder steady, allowing the smaller man to slide his other leg into the furred costume. The waist lifts easily, and Justin finds two shoulder straps tucked inside. He pulls them out and Aaron helps him adjust the height so the costume sits on his actual waist. As he pulls the second strap over his shoulder, something rolls out of the middle section of the costume and lands at his crotch. Justin looks down inside the costume, confused, and then surprised to see what looks like a dildo.

"No way," he breathes, snaking his arm inside the costume to pull it out. In the fluorescent lights of the locker room, he can see that it is about eight inches long and purple with a large wide base for easy gripping or using in a strap-on. He holds it up, looking at Aaron curiously. "Um?"

Aaron laughs, pushing his hand down and jamming the dildo back inside the costume. The quarterback smirks. "I'd just put that back where you found it," he says.

"Is this some kind of joke?" Justin asks, sliding the dildo back into a small pocket along the inside of the costume. The chest is larger than his own, loosely framed so there is plenty of room for the dildo without him feeling it. "Do I want to know?"

"Different strokes for different folks," Aaron says cryptically.

"Who wore this before me?"

"Someone who clearly liked to have a good time," Aaron says with a shrug. "I'd leave it alone."

Justin laughs, looking down at the furred costume covering him to mid chest. "I probably should have pissed before I got into this," he grumbles.

"No worries, mate," Aaron tells him, leaning down to flick a flap of fabric across the costume's crotch. "There's a flap here. Makes it much easier."

"That dildo suddenly makes a lot more sense," Justin comments, feeling around to get a sense of the flap. He has to pull down the horse's sewn-on gym shorts to access it, but there's plenty of room for his cock to go through it if he needs to.

Aaron frowns. "It also lets you get a breeze inside the costume occasionally. It's not too hot tonight, but sometimes that thing can be brutal." The quarterback gestures at the rest of the costume—a long-sleeved shirt of brown fur wearing a purple and silver Stallions jersey and a horse head fitted with what feels like a helmet inside. "You got this part or you need help?"

Justin nods. "I got this," he tells him. "But can you tell me if it's okay when it's all on?"

"Sure."

Justin reaches for the shirt, pleased to find that it doesn't smell bad when he tugs it over his head. They must have the costume cleaned regularly. He adjusts the shoulders, surprised to find that the material isn't that heavy. It's like a winter coat, and not entirely uncomfortable. He tugs the plush horse head over his head, glad to see that it's easy to see out through the mouth. His fingers fumble for the clips to secure the head to the rest of the costume, and then everything settles into place. He jumps a little, testing the movement.

"Not bad," Aaron nods. "Can you do the dance?"

Justin sighs, but he steps away from the bench, launching into the hip-thrusting jig the mascot makes at every goal.

"That'll do," Aaron says, grabbing his shoulders and pointing him at the doorway to the practice field and beyond. "Go get 'em, Stallion. Eager fans await your presence!"

ustin raises his arms in a huge clap, rocking his hips in the goal dance as the Stallions score yet another touchdown. The crowd screams, the stadium echoing with excitement.

"And that's another victory for your XTC Stallions!" the announcer yells, and the crowd lets out another cheer. Justin pumps his fists, arms only starting to hurt from the evening's exertions. He didn't realize how much the mascot moved around during a game, jumping and dancing and keeping the crowd going the entire time.

He is absolutely earning his extra points with all of this. He really wants to reach inside the horse's mouth and brush his sweaty hair out of his face, but he doesn't want to freak out any of the kids in the audience.

The game ends with a final whistle, and Justin spends the next half hour giving high fives and posing for selfies as the crowd slowly leaves the stands. The players are long gone, disappeared to the locker room for showers and gone to the after party. Justin thinks he can probably go to the celebration and debates how tired he is. He does not miss the irony that his extra credit for gym class is definitely a workout.

When no one else remains in the stands, he makes his way slowly back to the locker room. There is still steam in the air, remnants of the last showers, but the room is empty, a few stray towels lingering on the benches for someone else to pick up. Justin walks over to the bench and sits down, legs relieved to rest after the constant motion of the last three hours. He finds the buckles connecting the horse head to his shoulders and releases one. One arm is still inside the costume when a stern voice makes him freeze.

"Did I say you were finished, Mr. Cooper?"

Justin snaps his head up, the horse head lolling a bit to one side as one buckle is undone, but Coach Smith doesn't seem to mind. She is elated, her face glowing in satisfaction. She still wears her ball cap over that glorious red hair and a purple and silver jacket over her normal shirt and skirt.

"What else do you need, Coach Smith?" His hand moves to his pants, sliding down the waistband of his shorts.

She studies him, lips pursing as she takes a few slow steps closer to where he sits. She takes off her hat first, letting it fall to the floor and releasing her hair in a wave. Justin stares at her, cock growing hard at the memory of their last encounter.

"I'm not sure you're up to the task," she says with a frown, a finger lingering on the zipper of her jacket. She tugs it down slowly, and Justin grows harder as he realizes that she must have taken off her shirt at some point during the evening, the jacket falling aside to reveal two bare breasts with tight nipples. He remembers how she wasn't wearing panties when he went to visit her in the office, and he hopes she is bare this time too. He grips his cock, pulling it free of his shorts and giving a few short pumps.

"I can do anything you need me to," he promises, voice husky through the mask.

"I think you might do better without as much stimulation," she says, sliding the jacket off slowly, knowing his eyes are on every inch of revealed skin. "Let's see how well you can control yourself." The jacket hits the floor, and she stands in front of him wearing a tiny white pleated skirt. "A little test first, though." She reaches down, easily sliding the costume's shorts out of the way and lifting the strategically placed flap. Justin is expecting her, so his cock stands free of his own shorts, poking proudly through the hole in the costume.

She nods approvingly. "A promising start," she says, "but that was true last time too." She frowns. "Can you handle a little more excitement?" She turns around, lifting her skirt slowly to reveal first the long lines of her thighs and finally the curve of her ass. Justin's cock jerks in response to the sight, a drop of pre-cum shiny on the tip. She turns to frown down at him, shaking her head. "Mr. Cooper, you must control yourself."

"I am," he insists, "but you are so fucking hot right now."

Coach Smith smiles at him, a finger in her mouth as she sucks the tip. "You cannot come yet," she demands.

"Yes, ma'am," he replies, steeling himself.

She lifts a long leg, draping it over the bench and wrapping it around the back of the costume. She lowers herself slowly onto his cock, her other leg stretching over his to kneel on the bench. Justin moans as her warmth enfolds him, his free arm reaching around to feel her breasts. She knocks his arm down as she settles herself on his cock. "No," she tells him. "No touching. Just this."

Justin closes his eyes, not wanting to lose the sight of her breasts through the opening of the horse's mouth, but unable to focus on anything but the feel of that warm pussy on his cock, the only part of her touching his body. It's an odd sensation.

He can feel her weight on his legs, the motion of the costume's fabric as she slowly moves up and down, but he can't feel any part of her except the warm tightness over his cock.

"Fucking christ," he moans, hand lifting again to touch her as he opens his eyes to watch the beautiful woman riding him. She grabs the arm and pins it to his side, using it to hold as she moves up and down a little faster, breasts rising and falling with each bounce.

"Fucking Coach," she corrects, leaning back with her eyes closed, relishing the moment.

"Yes, ma'am," he says again, soaking in the sight as she leans back a little, breasts bouncing more as she increases her speed again. Justin can tell she is close to the edge, and he slides his other hand down again, slipping it out of the flap just enough for his thumb to press against her clit the next time she slides down his cock. Her eyes fly open and she stares at him through the mask, grinding her hips against his thumb with each thrust down.

"You naughty boy!" she exclaims, driving her body onto his cock. "You're going to make me come!" she yells, body shuddering against his. She pumps her hips a few more times, then sags against him, breath ragged as she sits, his hard cock still deep inside of her. "Nicely done, Mr. Cooper," she tells him when she sits up, wrapping her other leg around his hip and hooking her feet over his butt.

"I think you've earned a little reward," she says. "What would you like for your efforts?"

Justin stands up, snaking his hand outside of the costume so he can use both arms to hold her steady on his cock as he maneuvers around the costume, trying to get a feel for the weight distribution. "I want to fuck you silly," he says, spinning around and taking a few steps to press her back against the locker room wall. The motion makes it much easier to hold her, the costume bunched up just enough to hold her in place as he moves his hips for a slow first thrust back and forth. She lets out a moan, head ducked into the shoulder of the costume.

Justin squares his feet, settling into a medium pace, letting the friction build again as he pumps into her. "Fuck you are so tight," he moans.

"That cock is so big," she says. "And you move just right!"

"Are you going to come on this big cock?" he asks, thrusting from a slightly different angle. The noise she makes lets him know he has found the spot, and he focuses his efforts on hitting it every time he slides into her.

"Keep doing that!" she demands, body clinging to his, muscles trembling as she approaches the edge again. "Fuck yes!" she yells, body convulsing around his.

Justin nearly loses it, but he manages to hold himself back, thrusting a few more times as she squeezes him tight and then holding her steady, letting her shuddering body relax.

"Well done, Mr. Cooper," she says in a ragged voice. "I didn't think you had it in you."

"I believe it's in you, Coach Smith," he says, lifting her away from the wall and allowing her to slide off his cock to slowly stand on shaky legs. "Or it will be," he adds, hands on her shoulders to push her gently down on the bench. She kneels, perfect ass facing him as her skirt flips up over her hips. She turns around to see him, eyes dark over her shoulder and she bites her lip.

"Fuck me again, Mr. Cooper," she demands. "And this time, you're allowed to come. But only after I do."

"Greedy woman," Justin tells her, stepping forward to grab the line of her skirt, using the material to tug her ass back to him, her wet pussy enfolding his hard cock. He looks down, marveling at the idea of his cock inside of his teacher, the costume still between them. She presses back against him, moaning as he pulls back and watches his cock disappear inside her pussy again, pink lips sliding along the shaft. "Is this what you want?" he demands, pounding into her harder, losing sight of his cock as he looks up over the curve of her ass to see her head, hair in disarray over her face. "You like this cock, Coach Smith?"

"Oh yes!" she cries, ass pushing back against him. "Fuck me with that cock, Mr. Cooper!"

He uses one hand on the skirt to set the rhythm, pleasure building in his lower belly, then smacks her ass with the other, goading her on to move faster, harder. Finally, he lets go, pounding into her with abandon, both of them shouting their pleasure. Her body shudders around him, and he jerks, pouring himself deep inside of her as he comes. He pauses, then sags forward, body awkwardly draped over her back as he waits for his heart to calm back down to normal pace.

"Well, Mr. Cooper," she breathes, "it turns out you can go the distance on occasion."

4

"I cannot believe I'm doing this," Jamie Cooper complains, walking through the sliding doors into the XTC Stallions Athletic Center. "Twin brothers are the absolutely worst. He so owes me one for this. Big time."

She scans the entryway, glad to see that no one is around. Justin insisted that she wouldn't be seen at this time. She could come in, grab the costume, get dressed for the game on Friday back in her room, and cover for him so he could get his A in gym class.

"I can't believe you agreed to be the mascot," she told her brother. "That seems like a lot more effort than you normally put forth."

"You'd be surprised," Justin replied, smirking with some hidden joke. Jamie doesn't want to know. She wants to get into the locker room, grab the costume, and get back to her room before anyone notices.

She opens the locker room door slowly, listening intently for any noise. Hearing none, she steps inside, sneakers quiet on the tile floor. The mascot costume sits where Justin said it would be, propped up on the corner of the bench across the room, the horse head sitting next to the other pieces. Frowning, Jamie considers the costume. She can put it on and walk across campus without too much comment. There isn't a game until tomorrow, but Justin can't let any of the players see that he has his sister covering for him, so she needs to get into costume elsewhere.

She listens for another moment, hearing nothing, and walks closer to the costume. Lifting the pants, she frowns again.

Justin, you owe me big time, she thinks with a sigh, putting the costume on the ground and stepping into one leg. She wobbles dangerously when she tries to put in her other leg but catches herself against the bench just in time. The shoulder straps are the right height—she and Justin are the same size—so it's easy to put them on. She tugs the shirt over her head, pleasantly surprised by the fresh smell. They must dry clean the costume often.

She adjusts the shirt, then finds the clips along the shoulders, no doubt meant to connect to the head. Sighing, she lifts up the head, staring into the long partially open mouth.

"Fuck my life," she groans, resting the head on top of her own, balancing the awkward weight. She finds one clip and secures a side, but then there are voices just outside the door.

Jamie panics, not sure what to do. In a flurry, she whirls around to face the door. The weight of the costume knocks her off balance and she stumbles backward, landing awkwardly in the corner of the room, but landing heavily on the bench. The horse head slides to one side and she slides her arms inside the costume to catch it, not caring if the shoulder straps fall off her shoulders. The shirt covers her body. She drags the head back into place and then sags back, praying that the costume looks like someone left it that way on purpose, leaning into the corner, as the door opens.

A blonde girl walks in, flanked by three men, clearly players. Jamie recognizes the twins Bryan and Ryan from her sociology class. The third guy is vaguely familiar, like she's seen him at the Tutoring Center before, but she can't place his name.

Fuck, she thinks, watching the group as they chat for a moment, something about studying for finals, body tense as she stays motionless inside the costume. *Good, if they're getting ready to go study, they won't stay very long.*

Her hopes for a quick exit are dashed when Aaron, the gorgeous quarterback who has starred in more than one of her shower fantasies, comes inside. His words make something quiver deep inside Jamie. She doesn't believe what she sees at first, sure that her oversexed mind is reading into the body language of the people in the gym, but when Aaron leans in and asks, "What do you think?" in that sexy voice, Jamie wants to scream at the propositioned blonde, "Say yes! Dear god say yes!"

The eight guys surround the blonde and lead her into the shower, presumably a reward for her getting the answer on her study card right.

Oh wow, Jamie thinks, not really believing what she's seeing until Aaron leans down to kiss her while the big guy slides his hands into the girl's pants. Her own hand drifts lower on her belly, wishing she could have so many hands on her body at one time. The two guys undress the blonde, revealing a body that makes Jamie question her orientation. She's made out with girls before, but she tends to prefer cock—this woman might satisfy her without one.

Jamie's hand moves lower, sliding along the edge of her gym shorts, teasing her skin as she watches. When the boys carry the girl—Bree, she knows now, she's heard them whisper her name a few times—into the shower and she begins stroking the red-head's cock, Jamie sighs, shifting her body slightly so she can get her hand inside of her pants. Her touch is gentle at first, teasing as she watches Bree stroke the men in the shower, taking turns kissing them. But when Aaron kneels to bury his face in the blonde's pussy, Jamie's hand becomes more insistent, pressing hard with a soft jerk against the side of the mascot, and something falls out of a pocket to tumble onto her lap. Jamie freezes, wondering if anyone saw the movement.

Desperate cries echo from the shower, and she sighs in relief, knowing that no one would be watching this side of the room with that show in front of them. She's fascinated too.

Her hand pulls out of her pants, curious about the object that she dislodged. Her fingers locate the soft silky texture of a long firm object, and she drops the item in shock. It lands against her belly, surface silicone smooth, and she reaches for it again, surprise giving way to excitement.

Of course, she thinks. *Of course there's a dildo inside the mascot. Why wouldn't there be?*

She turns her attention back to the shower, angling her head so she can see around the bulk of the twins who stand partially blocking the opening. She can see that the girl is on the floor now, head thrown back as her body moves rhythmically, no doubt fucking one of the lucky players. Jamie's hand snakes inside her pants again, imagining that she is in that shower, men surrounding her as she rides Aaron's cock all the way home. Her body grows tight, and she closes her eyes, caught in the fantasy as her fingers press hard against her clit. She holds in a moan as the pleasure builds, shuddering as the wave crashes over her, hand relaxing on her clit as the orgasm ebbs.

She opens her eyes again, this time seeing the woman held up by the guys, hands rubbing her body, a face buried between her thighs again. Jamie brushes against her clit again, watching intently, knowing that her second orgasm is always much faster and more powerful than the first. The pleasure floods her, and then she sags back.

The water turning off has her opening her eyes again, and she watches, expecting the party to be over. To her surprise, the guys carry the blonde over to the massage table, where she climbs to all fours so one player can fuck her while she sucks the other's cock.

Jamie's hand drifts over the dildo, wishing she could have a cock inside her too.

Oh no, she thinks wickedly. *I can't.*

But when the player flips Bree over and sheaths himself in one move, powerful body moving against hers, Jamie decides that she can. She moves the dildo slowly, sliding the length so it's even with her thighs at first, then slips it between her shorts and her leg, hiking up her shorts as she goes. The head is thick, but her pussy is wet when she reaches it, sliding her panties aside easily to rest the dildo against her opening.

Bree is moaning on the table, clearly about to come again, and Jamie presses the dildo in, just a little bit, letting her body accept the width. Her other hand moves to stroke her clit again, pressing down hard as she slowly moves on the dildo.

The players have swapped again, this time with one between Bree's legs while the other straddles her and fucks her gorgeous breasts. The other guys are kneeling around her, hands pumping hard cocks.

This is fucking amazing, Jamie thinks, squeezing her pussy on the dildo, taking a little more inside of her with each moan from the table. *Or amazing fucking!*

She is about to come, but then a door slams, and Coach Smith walks into the room. Jamie freezes, heart pounding, sure they are all going to get in trouble. But when the Coach simply climbs on the table to sit on Bree's face, Jamie loses control, sliding her small body up and down on the dildo and rubbing her clit furiously, coming hard and fast, her own pleasure lost in the general chorus of moans coming from the other side of the table.

Jamie recovers enough to hear Bree's last words: "Best. Studygroup. Ever." They don't take long after that, quick showers and friendly banter as they all head out of the locker room.

She waits until the room is empty, moving her stuff muscles slowly. She slides the dildo out of her pussy, echoes of pleasure streaking through her, and gets slowly to her feet.

Bree is so right. That was the best study session ever. Jamie doesn't think she will ever forget the names of the body systems with such excellent visual aids.

amie raises her arms, encouraging the crowd to whoop in time with the music as Aaron throws yet another winning touchdown. She has been in the costume for a few hours, but no one seems to notice that she isn't Justin. She is tired, her body in shape but exhausted by the effort of moving the heavy horse head around the crowd. She performs the dancing jig that accompanies the goal, but the muscles in her stomach and thighs protest, not used to the motion.

She can't wait to get back to the locker room and take off the costume. She plans to leave it on the bench in the locker room, slipping out unnoticed after the players finish up.

She lingers with the crowd after the game, giving Aaron's blonde head a lingering gaze as he leaves the field, carried along in the swell of his fan's adoration.

Some day, she thinks, *I will have that boy.*

With a sigh, she walks slowly back to the locker room, hoping that the players will all be on to the afterparty by now. When she walks in, the room is dark, the sensor lights turned off after a period with no motion. Jamie sighs in relief, moving to the corner bench where she found the mascot the first time

27

she came in the locker room. The lights turn on as she enters, the room flooded as she moves, and Coach Smith is sitting on the bench in the corner, legs spread wide along each length of wood, skirt flipped up to reveal her bare pussy. Her hands work slow circles on her clit, her skin flushed pink.

"You certainly took your time, Mr. Cooper," Coach Smith says with a languid smile. "I've done most of the work for you already."

Jamie freezes, knowing that she cannot speak or risk giving her brother away. *You freaking idiot*, she thinks angrily. *It's not enough that you dicked around and now need to be the mascot for the grade you need, but now you're fucking the teacher?* She takes a deep breath, squaring her shoulders inside the suit, knowing what her brother would do in this situation. They are twins, after all. Justin can't be that different from her in bed.

Fuck, she thinks, eyes widening as she takes a few steps toward the coach. *She's expecting me to fuck her again. I may be willing to go fairly far to help out my brother, but my willingness isn't going to give me a dick!*

She reaches the bench, appreciating the welcoming smile on Coach Smith's face. She's seen the coach join in on the gang bang with Bree, so she has an idea what the beautiful woman considers a good time. Jamie raises her arms to the horse head, undoing one of the straps and tilting the head to the side, moving it so the lower part of her face is visible through the mouth. The head is still shadowed, and they look enough alike that the coach should not be able to tell it's not Justin.

Dammit Justin, can't you just do your regular work? Now I have to earn your extra credit! As she takes in the lines of the coach's svelte body, Jamie decides that it's not a complete hardship. Coach Smith is smoking hot. Jamie is willing to take one for the team.

She gets to her knees, reaching out to caress the coach with her gloved hands, sliding the furry suit against the coach's slick wetness. Jamie suddenly knows why this suit smells so good. It must get cleaned fairly regularly after being used like this. She wonders how many students have worn it, how many have earned extra points by pleasuring the coach this way. Coach Smith moans, looking down at where Jamie kneels in appreciation. "Determined to get caught up, are we?" she asks. "Don't worry. I have plenty more left in me."

Jamie focuses on her work, rubbing her paws against the Coach the way she enjoys being touched, reading the woman's body for cues. Leaning down, she lifts one of the Coach's legs over her shoulder, bringing her mouth to the warm skin of her clit. It's not the first time she's licked pussy, and it probably won't be the last. Jamie enjoys sex of all kinds, though in the end, she prefers a good hard cock to end the encounter. She feels herself getting wet as she buries her tongue in the coach's slick folds, still using her hands to rub slow circles over her clit.

"Oh, Mr. Cooper!" Coach Smith yells. "You've been practicing!"

Jamie restrains a chuckle, her warm breath puffing out to stimulate the Coach's smooth skin, and she presses down on the clit more firmly, sensing the coach is close. She has wrapped her other leg around the back of Jamie's neck, the horse head sliding but not in danger of falling off as she presses closer.

Coach Smith moans as her body tightens, the orgasm spilling through her. Jamie gives her a moment to catch her breath, but then dives back in, knowing that the second orgasm is often easier than the first, and sometimes more powerful when combined with the effects of the first one so soon after. The coach stiffens against Jamie's mouth, coming again and shuddering against her face. She leans back after that, body falling limp to lean against the corner, small breasts heaving as she catches her breath.

"Mr. Cooper," she says after a moment, eyes narrowed, "you have been paying attention." She removes her leg from Jamie's shoulder and slides down to sit on Jamie's lap, eager mouth finding Jamie's under the mask, their heads tilted just enough so the coach can't see the rest of her face. Jamie returns the kiss, enjoying the coach's mouth, letting her hands slide over pert breasts and then down to hold her hips.

She drags out the kiss, mind frantically running through options for the next step. Coach Smith's hands begin working at the shorts, and Jamie remembers the dildo at the last second. She slides a hand back inside the costume, hoping the coach will think she's adjusting her clothes, and grabs the dildo, positioning it with her hand so it faces the right direction. She sucks the coach's tongue into her mouth as she does so, distracting the woman long enough for Jamie to slide the flap aside and use her hand to find her dripping pussy. The coach doesn't wait, following Jamie's hand back to slide down the length of the dildo, rocking her hips forward as she does so. The base of the dildo presses against Jamie's clit, and she stifles a moan. Her hand returns to the base, and she grips it hard, determined to keep the dildo steady as Coach Smith begins to move up and down.

The sight is delightful, Coach Smith's breasts bouncing up and down just below Jamie's eye level, her chest flushed with passion, soft gasps of pleasure escaping her lips as she increases her speed. "Cooper," she says, "you are so hard for me tonight!"

Jamie bites her lip, the pressure of the dildo base and her own hand rubbing her clit in all the right ways. She begins to breathe more heavily, and pitching her voice low like Justin's, she lets a small moan escape.

"Oh yes!" Coach Smith moans, body moving hard and fast now. "Come for me!"

Jamie rocks her hips up, hoping the coach will think Justin is coming, and she lets out a low hitching moan. Coach puts her hands on Jamie's shoulders and leans back, her entire body shuddering as she rides herself over the edge. Her body collapses against the furry chest of the costume, and they stay that way for a moment, both breathing hard—coach from her orgasm, Jamie from frustration. The dildo has gotten her close, but it's not enough. She needs just a little bit more.

Coach Smith stands up slowly, and Jamie is quick to yank the dildo back inside, folding the flap back into place before the woman can look down. The coach smiles, nods, and takes a few steps across the room. She turns back to where Jamie still kneels on the floor.

"Nicely done, Cooper," Coach Smith. "I think you've definitely earned that A!"

*J*amie waits for Coach Smith to leave the locker room, then stands up on shaky legs, turns around, and plops on the bench. She hears the door of the coach's office open and shut, and then there is no more noise. Jamie rests, catching her breath and letting her heart slow back down, very aware of the frustrated tension in her lower belly. She tucks the dildo back inside the suit, knowing that whoever gets it cleaned will take care of it, then rests her hand on top of her pussy, finger idly toying with her clit.

She contemplates rubbing herself to orgasm quickly, but then frowns. She really wants to get out of the costume. She abandons her clit, using both hands to undo the second clip on the horse head, and she takes it off with a sigh, her sweaty hair falling in her face as she rests it on the bench next to her.

"No fucking way," a voice says, and she jerks her head up to see Aaron, star quarterback and gorgeous blonde, staring at her from where he has entered the locker room. He narrows his eyes at her. "You're not Justin."

Jamie bites her lip, not sure what to say. She doesn't remember if Justin and Aaron are close friends or not.

Aaron looks from her to the hallway where the coach disappeared a while ago and then back at her. "You're not Justin," he says again, head cocking to the side, "but you just fucked Coach." He pauses, then adds, "And did a damn good job of it, judging by her expression when she walked out of here."

Jamie smiles brightly at him, deciding to brazen it out. "I have some skills," she says.

"Does one of those skills involve a cock?" he asks. "Because I'm pretty sure she was riding you a little while ago."

Jamie looks down, biting her bottom lip hard, unable to speak, not sure what to say. She wasn't expecting her first conversation with Aaron to involve him asking if she had a cock. "I...uh...have lots of skills?" she says eventually, voice shy as she looks away.

Aaron chuckles, walking over to sit on the bench next to her. He leans back against the wall. "So you're Justin's sister, right? Jamie?"

Jamie smiles, surprised that he knows her name. She nods. "And you're Aaron," she says.

He looks her up and down in the costume, a slow grin crossing his face. "Wanna tell me what's going on?"

Jamie shrugs. "Brothers are a huge pain in the ass?"

Aaron laughs. "True. But sisters are awesome," he says, flashing her a charming smile, "especially smoking hot ones."

Jamie raises an eyebrow, not buying it. Her hair is plastered to her head from wearing the horse head. Her mouth is still shiny with Coach Smith's wetness. She's flushed and flustered and sitting in most of a mascot costume next to the object of her crush.

"Yeah, right," she says, rolling her eyes and running a hand through her hair. "Nothing about me is smoking right now."

"You are a delicious hot mess," he says, leaning closer to her. "But you must be dying in that costume. How about I help you take it off?"

Jamie nods, face warming at the idea of Aaron helping her take off any kind of clothing.

He turns to her, grabbing her arm first and sliding off one glove. He sets it to the side then scoots closer to her, hands reaching for her other arm, and making a face when he realizes that one of her sleeves is empty, the hand already inside the costume. "Arms up?" he suggests, and Jamie lifts her one arm, letting him tug the shirt over her head. She sighs with relief as the cool air hits her flushed skin, setting the shirt on the bench next to the rest of the costume. "Better?" he asks.

"Much," she nods, but looks down at herself. "But I need to get out of the rest of this."

"Happy to help," he says, moving closer to slide the shoulder strap off her arm, hands lingering on her skin as he moves it down. He pushes the other strap to the side, and the costume sinks, falling to puddle around her waist. Jamie lifts both arms up, stretching tired muscles, and Aaron moves closer, grabbing her gently about the hips and tugging her legs up on the bench, sliding her body so she now sits with her back to one wall, the left side of her body touching the other wall. He slides the pants off one leg at a time, helping to lift her hips off the bench so the costume can slip free. Jamie is very aware of what she is wearing underneath, a simple tank top and small bootie shorts.

Aaron smiles at her, tossing the remains of the costume on top of the pile on the other side of her. "Better?"

"Definitely."

He lifts both of her legs so they rest on top of his lap, scooting closer on the bench until he turns his body, and leans forward, a hand capturing her chin and tilting her face up to him.

"You are so hot," he breathes. "Can I kiss you?"

"Fuck yeah," Jamie says, closing the distance between their faces, mouth claiming his fiercely, knowing thet she still tastes of Coach Smith's pussy, knowing that Aaron will enjoy her kiss even more. She puts a hand on the back of his neck, pulling him closer and urging him on, the frustration in her body surging to the surface. One of his hands slides down from her face to cup the outside of her shoulder and then slides down her arm, moving more slowly as he gets near her breasts.

The heat in Jamie's belly pulses, and she grabs his hand and jams it to her breast, encouraging him even more. He pulls away slightly, breath still a whisper on her lips, "You want me?"

"I want you to fuck me sideways and silly," she tells him, biting his lower lip with hers. "I'm so fucking horny right now. I need you inside of me!"

Aaron grins, hands slipping down to tug off her shorts.

"Happy to help!" His hands return to her pussy immediately, sliding against her wet heat. "Fuck, Jamie," he moans, burying fingers inside of her slick warmth.

"Yes," she tells him, "please fuck Jamie."

He grins again, hand moving faster, breath against her mouth. "I am so glad you don't have a cock right now."

"No cock yet," she tells him, hands reaching to tug his pants off, "but I hope to have one soon." She pauses long enough to let him take off his shirt, hands tugging from behind his neck in that adorable way men always take off shirts. His clothes land on the floor, and then she is climbing on top of him. She wants to ride him the way the coach rode her dildo.

He stops her with firm hands on her hips, sliding her closer to him, her bare thighs rubbing against the tops of his legs, and his huge cock is hard, shaft rubbing against her clit as she presses her body close to his. She leans back as he scoots forward a little bit, giving her legs enough room to wrap around his waist.

Aaron leans forward, claiming her mouth again, rubbing his cock against the front of her pussy, the hard muscles of his abdomen pressing against her soft skin, his hand sliding up to pinch a nipple, the other reaching around to grip her ass. "You want this cock?" he asks, and Jamie moans in response.

"Please," she says finally, body aching with need.

He lifts her easily, hands guiding her body as she slips down the length of his shaft, the burning desire inside finally getting what she wants. "Yes," she says, moving her body slowly, relishing the feeling of fullness, the promise of satisfaction after so much buildup and tension. She moves slowly at first, hands holding his shoulders to help her set the rhythm, eager mouth moving against his. She finds a speed she likes and leans in close, releasing his mouth long enough to cry out her release.

"There you go," he says as she shudders against him. When she comes back to herself, he gives her a challenging grin. "I'm thinking about five more of those, and we should be somewhere close to where we need to be," he tells her.

"Only five?" she teases. "Why not six? That's a touchdown, at least."

Aaron smirks. "Then I should go for the extra point and call it seven," he promises, hands gripping her ass.

Jamie smiles at him, body beginning to move again. "Sounds good," she says, squeezing him tight inside. "And I expect every single one of them. Call it my extra credit."

ALI WHIPPE

A li Whippe is the pen name of a professor in the higher education system who delights in imagining naughty distractions while enduring endless mind-numbing committee meetings. She loves to push the boundaries of the written word and the imagination, knowing that life at work would be way more exciting if more people didn't wear panties.

Honey Cummings
Sleeping with Sasquatch
Cuddling with Chupacabra
Naked with New Jersey Devil
Laying with the Lady in Blue
Wanton Woman in White
Beating it with Bloody Mary

Beau and Professor Bestialora
The Goat's Gruff
Goldie and Her Three Beards
Pied Piper's Pipe
Princess Pea's Bed

LGBT Erotica

Grayson Ace
How I Got Here
First Year Out of the Closet
You're Only a Top?
You're Only a Bottom?
I Think I'm a Serial Swiper

Leo Sparx
Claiming Alexander
Taming Alexander
Saving Alexander

4HorsemenPublications.com